Ladies and Jellybeans

Ladies and Jellybeans

By Candice F. Ransom

Bradbury Press • New York

Maxwell Macmillan Canada • Toronto
Maxwell Macmillan International
New York • Oxford • Singapore • Sydney

Bradbury Press
Macmillan Publishing Company
866 Third Avenue
New York, NY 10022

Maxwell Macmillan Canada, Inc.
1200 Eglinton Avenue East
Suite 200
Don Mills, Ontario M3C 3N1

Macmillan Publishing Company is part of the Maxwell Communication
Group of Companies.

First edition
Printed and bound in the United States of America

10   9   8   7   6   5   4   3   2   1

The text of this book is set in 15 point Caledonia.

Library of Congress Cataloging-in-Publication Data
Ransom, Candice F., date–
Ladies and jellybeans / by Candice F. Ransom. — 1st ed.
p.   cm.
Summary: As Wendy starts the third grade in the late 1950s, she
worries about cursive writing, Show and Tell, the Cold War, and her
father's new job.
ISBN 0-02-775665-3
[1. Schools—Fiction.]   I. Title.
PZ7.R1743Lad   1991
[Fic]—dc20   91-14710

For my husband, Frank,
a perfect jellybean

Contents

CHAPTER ONE

First Day Worries

Wendy Fletcher gripped her new lunch-box nervously. It was time to leave for the bus. Wendy was starting third grade. She was both excited and scared.

Her second grade teacher, Miss Wells, had smelled like baby powder. Miss Wells said Wendy was the neatest printer in class. Wendy liked printing. Third graders were

1

supposed to learn cursive. What if she couldn't do real writing?

"Wendy, are you ready?" her sister, Denise, called. She clumped to the doorway of the kitchen in her new Buster Brown shoes.

Wendy looked down at her own shoes, old ones from last year. The laces were knotted because she still couldn't tie bows. For some reason, Wendy's feet didn't grow at all over the summer. "Thank heavens," Mrs. Fletcher had said in the shoe store the week before. "If you can make do until Christmas with your old shoes, it'll really help." Wendy didn't know what her mother was talking about, but she was glad to make her happy.

Denise's feet had grown two sizes. Wendy's sister wasn't pleased about her big feet. She was going to be a big-shot sixth grader and was sensitive about these things. "I'll be wearing the shoebox next," she'd grumbled.

"Let's go," Denise said now. "We'll miss the bus."

"Be good," Wendy's mother said, kissing Wendy. "Denise, watch your sister at the bus stop. Those big trucks—"

"Okay, okay." Denise was so impatient that Wendy wondered if her new shoes were still too tight.

"Did Daddy get my flower?" Wendy asked her mother.

"Yes. He said thanks."

It was Mr. Fletcher's first day, too—at a new job. He had left for work early, while Wendy was still in bed. The night before, she had placed a flower by his plate.

"Wendy, come *on!*" Denise was out the door.

Wendy ran to catch up. The two girls walked down the long driveway. They could hear birds singing in the woods that bordered their property. Wendy glanced over at the Martins' house, which she could see through the trees. Their nearest neighbor was three acres away, but sometimes Wendy glimpsed Mrs. Martin milking Daisy, her cow. This morning Wendy didn't even see the cow.

At the bottom of the driveway, they stopped to wait. "Stand back," Denise ordered.

"I *am* back."

Cars and trucks whooshed along Lee Highway. Wendy wondered if she would see her father go by in a flash of orange. As part of his new job, Mr. Fletcher drove a Virginia State truck.

"Do they have chocolate milk at ten

o'clock in third grade?" Wendy asked.

Denise frowned, as if trying to recall something long buried in her past. "I don't think so. Only the babies in first and second grade get a morning snack."

Wendy was glad that waiting until lunchtime to eat was the mark of an older kid. But she was disappointed that she wouldn't get chocolate milk anymore. The school's chocolate milk was a lot better than the kind they made at home. Denise never poured enough syrup in the glass, so the milk was a weak grayish color instead of a nice chocolaty brown.

"What about Sharing? Will we still have that?" Wendy hoped not. She didn't like getting up in front of the class. Anyway, she never had anything interesting to share.

"Honestly, Wendy. How do you expect me to remember all that stuff?" Importantly, Denise pulled a newspaper from her notebook.

Wendy read the big print: THE WASHINGTON POST, *Tuesday, September 4, 1959*. A smaller headline said: "Eisenhower to Meet with Cabinet." Wendy didn't know the president held meetings in the kitchen of the White House.

"We have current events in sixth grade," Denise boasted. "If my teacher asks me, I'm ready to talk about President Eisenhower's meeting."

"I hope we don't have current events," Wendy said. "I don't know anything about President Eisenhower's meeting in the kitchen."

Denise kicked at gravel with her new shoes. "Ladies and jellybeans!" she boomed. "I come before you to stand behind you to tell you something I know nothing about!"

Wendy chimed in, "I come behind you to stand before you—"

"That's not right," Denise said.

Wendy wanted to kick gravel, too, but then she remembered that her shoes had to last until Christmas. Denise was glad to be going to school, but Wendy was having second thoughts. No snack, no Miss Wells, no printing. Maybe she could convince her parents she really didn't *need* to go to school. After all, she could read and add and subtract and spell. What else was there to learn?

"Bus!" Denise bellowed as the familiar yellow shape nosed over the hill.

A new, bigger worry fluttered in Wendy's stomach. "I don't have a real friend," she said.

"What about Debbie?" Denise said as they climbed into the bus.

"She moved, remember? She doesn't go to our school anymore," Wendy said gloomily. "I won't know anybody."

"Sure you will. Some kids from last year will be in your class. You'll make new friends."

Easy for Denise to talk. Last year it had taken Wendy three weeks to say hello to Debbie Zirk. Debbie showed Wendy how to play jacks during recess. Wendy never got beyond "threesies," but she was happy that Debbie was her friend. Who would be her friend this year? A real friend—somebody she could play with during recess and sit with at lunch. Over the summer, Wendy had had no one to play with except Denise. A school friend was more important than *any*thing.

At Warrensville Elementary School, Denise took Wendy to her new room. A few days ago, Wendy's parents got the letter saying Wendy would be in Mrs. Boggs's class, Room 5. "I'll meet you here after school so you won't get on the wrong bus," Denise told her sister, then ran up the stairs to her sixth grade room.

The last bell rang. Kids who were playing outside on the blacktop streamed through the doors. They chattered about which teachers they had this year. Wendy saw some kids from her class last year going into Room 6, Miss Kline's room, the other third grade class.

Her new teacher was sitting behind her desk when Wendy walked in. Wendy sniffed. Mrs. Boggs wasn't wearing baby powder.

"Take any seat you wish," she said. "I don't believe in assigning seats right away."

A teacher who didn't believe in assigned

seats! Wendy decided she liked Mrs. Boggs, even if she didn't smell like baby powder. She looked around. Buses were rolling in late from the back roads around Warrensville, so kids were still arriving. There were a lot of new faces, military kids who had moved to Warrensville over the summer. Wendy saw only two people from Miss Wells's room. She hoped she wouldn't have to make brand-new friends from scratch.

She chose a desk beside a boy with curly blond hair. The astonishing thing about this boy was that he was wearing shorts and a white shirt with a striped tie. All the other boys were wearing pants and clean, pressed shirts. Nobody had on a tie.

Wendy stared. She had never seen anyone dressed this way before. Did he realize he had on shorts? Maybe he put them on by mistake. And why was he wearing a tie? It wasn't Sunday. She decided he must have to go someplace important right after school, like the doctor's. She felt a little sorry for him.

The boy felt her stare. "Hi," he said. "Are you new here?"

Wendy wasn't sure what he meant. Everyone in Mrs. Boggs's class was new. None of them had ever been in this room before. Unless he was a left-back. That must be it. He was repeating third grade.

"I'm sorry you failed," she said finally. "I bet you couldn't learn cursive, could you?"

The boy scowled at her. "I didn't fail! And I can write cursive. I just came here from Bamberg, Germany. We lived there for three years. I can sing 'Jingle Bells' in German."

Wendy had only been as far as the Great

Smoky Mountains. She glanced at the world map hanging on the wall. Was Germany that big pink country above the United States? No, that was Canada. "Is Germany across the ocean?" she asked.

"Of course," the boy replied. "We had to fly to get here."

She looked at him, impressed. Imagine, flying in an airplane! She didn't know anyone who had flown in an airplane. She forgot her shyness, wanting to hear more about this boy. "My name is Wendy. What's yours?"

"Nelson."

She giggled. "That sounds like your last name!"

"Well, it isn't. My whole name is Nelson James Andrews the Fourth."

"The fourth what?"

"The fourth person in my family to have

that name," he said, annoyed. "My father was named Nelson James Andrews and so was my grandfather and my great-grandfather."

Wendy figured the people in Nelson's family couldn't think of new names, so they gave their kids the same one over and over. Then she noticed a leather bag leaning against his desk. It had straps and buckles and three gold letters—NJA—stamped on the handle.

"Is that your lunchbox?" she asked admiringly.

Nelson followed her gaze. "Nah. That's my bookbag. I got it when we were on vacation in Denmark. All the Danish kids have them."

Maybe the people in Nelson's family weren't very smart, but Nelson Andrews was just about the smartest person Wendy had ever met. She didn't have anything as fancy as a Danemark bookbag. She showed him her Mickey Mouse Club lunchbox, how the thermos fit in a spring-loaded wire that kept it from rolling around.

"Neat," Nelson said. "I missed American TV shows when we were in Germany. And hamburgers! The first thing that we did when we landed in America was go to the drive-in."

Now she knew why Nelson was wearing short pants. His long pants were probably still packed.

As more buses arrived, students trickled into the room. A girl with brownish-red braids claimed the seat in front of Wendy. She turned and said, "I remember you. You were in Miss Wells's room last year."

Wendy remembered the girl, too. Her name was Regina Coopersmith. Wendy was relieved to see someone from her old room. Then Wayne Supinger came in. He'd been in Wendy's old room, too, but Wendy didn't like him much. Wayne took a desk way in the back, where he could cut up.

Another girl sat on the other side of Wendy. Her yellow stringy hair fell over her eyes, which were pale blue. Her shoes were "eating her socks," as Wendy's mother would say. Wendy checked her own socks to make sure they were still up.

Mrs. Boggs took attendance. Nelson's name was called first.

He leaped to stand beside his desk and cried, "Present," in a clear, ringing voice. Wayne and the other boys snickered.

Mrs. Boggs said, "In our school, Nelson, it isn't necessary to stand when you are called on."

"Oh." Nelson sat down stiffly. A dull red flush crept up over his ears. Wendy felt sorry for him. She knew what it was like to be embarrassed in front of other kids.

"Kristy Bostic," Mrs. Boggs called.

The girl with the stringy yellow hair whispered, "Here."

"Robert Bowers."

A boy in the back yelled, "Present!" The other boys laughed again.

Mrs. Boggs gave them a look. "Sandra Eagen."

Wendy remembered the small girl who answered "Here" from Miss Wells's class. Sandra was a whole year younger than the others, but she had been to private kindergarten.

"Wendy Fletcher."

"Present." Wendy decided she liked the crisp way the word sounded. Nelson looked at her. She smiled, so he wouldn't think she was making fun of him, too.

Mrs. Boggs started talking about the work they would do that year. They would have Sharing, but not every day. Only once in a while, whenever someone had something special to talk about.

Wendy gnawed a thumbnail. Would they have to write cursive right away? She wanted to ask, but was afraid to raise her hand. Once her second grade teacher sent a note home: "Wendy does not volunteer answers in class."

Now Mrs. Boggs walked up and down the aisles, passing out plain file folders. Wendy had been so worried about cursive and volunteering answers that she hadn't heard a word the teacher said.

She poked Regina Coopersmith. "What did she say?" she whispered.

"We're going to make folders to put our best work in," Regina replied over her shoulder. "Weren't you paying attention?"

"I didn't hear her."

Just then Mrs. Boggs handed Wendy her folder. She smiled, revealing a dimple. Wendy liked teachers who smiled. Miss Wells had been a smiley teacher. Her first grade teacher, Mrs. Foster, had been an old grouch. Two smiley teachers in a row was a good sign.

"This will be your Best Work folder," Mrs. Boggs told the class. "Decorate it any way you wish. I have supplies up here. Make your folder special, so everybody knows it's yours."

Wendy had a new box of crayons. Her mother had bought her a big box with sixty-four colors and a built-in sharpener when they bought Denise's shoes. She began drawing Birdland. In second grade she used to draw Birdland whenever Miss Wells gave them free time.

Wendy loved birds. She watched them all the time, out the window of her class, at the bus stop, in her front yard. She was fascinated by their different shapes and colors.

First she drew an enormous tree with spreading branches. Then she drew birdhouses along the branches. A church birdhouse perched next to the school birdhouse, which had a bell on top. The grocery store birdhouse had tiny little carts out front. There was even a First National Birdland Bank. Brightly colored birds hopped busily up and down the branch-streets.

Every time she drew Birdland, she made it bigger and more fantastic. It was her favorite thing in the world to draw. She wished she lived in Birdland. The city she made up was much nicer than the country, where she lived. Wendy longed to have friends next door, like on TV.

Kristy Bostic, the stringy-haired girl with the falling socks across from her, borrowed crayons from the teacher. She colored a scribbly sunset on her folder. Wendy noticed that Kristy didn't draw very well. Nelson's picture of an airplane was pretty good, though.

"This is the plane we flew home in," he said. "A DC-6."

Regina turned around in her seat to show Wendy her folder. "See my chinchilla? My dad raises them—we have over a hundred. But Fluffy is mine."

"Fluffy," Nelson scoffed. "How original."

"You don't even know what a chinchilla

is," Regina fired back, her eyes blazing.

"I do, too," Nelson replied airily. "My mother has a chinchilla fur coat. They're little animals you kill and sew into coats. You ought to be ashamed."

"My father takes very good care of our chinchillas," Regina retorted. "We don't kill them. He sends them away and these other people—" She broke off.

Kristy and Nelson stared at Regina. Wendy knew what they were thinking, that other people killed the chinchillas for their fur.

She tried to patch the awkward silence. "I think Fluffy is a nice name. If I had a chinchilla, that's what I'd name him."

Regina's face brightened. "He *is* fluffy." But she was still angry at Nelson. "How come you're wearing shorts?" she demanded.

Nelson shaded the wings of his airplane with a skinny yellow pencil, the kind big kids used. "I'll have you know these are short *pants*. That's what boys in Europe wear to school."

"Well, you're not in Europe, wherever that is," Regina stated flatly. "You're in Warrensville and I think you look dumb. So there."

Wendy was surprised to see tears in Nelson's eyes. She didn't think smart kids ever had their feelings hurt.

"That's okay," she whispered to him. "You'll get your long pants unpacked and wear them tomorrow. I bet your folder is the best one."

"You think so?" Then he looked over at her folder. "What's yours supposed to be?"

"Birdland. It's sort of a town for birds. Here's the school. . . ."

Regina and Kristy listened, too. Wendy was surprised they seemed really interested.

"I like your picture," Kristy said shyly. "Are you going to be an artist?"

"I don't know," Wendy replied. But she was pleased. Kristy thought she was good enough to be an artist!

When everyone had finished decorating their folders, Mrs. Boggs collected the crayons and paste and unused construction paper.

"Now I want you to write your name on the tab," she said.

Regina raised her hand. Wendy was amazed at the way Regina just threw up her arm and waggled her fingers. Regina was like Denise, bold and unafraid.

"Writing or printing, Mrs. Boggs?" Regina asked.

"I'm sorry. I should have been more clear. Print your name for now. We won't be learning cursive until we order our workbooks."

Wendy happily selected her favorite crayon, blue-green. She printed her name— "Wendy F."—perfectly, making the circles round as apples and the stick-parts straight as trees.

Wendy held up her folder. Secretly she thought it was the nicest folder in the class, even better than Nelson's. She couldn't wait to show it to Denise.

Soon it would be recess and then, lunchtime. It was hard to believe she had three new almost-friends to play with. She wouldn't have to answer questions, either, not with Regina Coopersmith in front of her and so quick to raise her hand. Best of all, she wouldn't have to write cursive for a very long, long time.

Maybe she had worried over nothing. So far, third grade was a cinch.

CHAPTER TWO

The Tight Year

By the end of the second week, Wendy loved third grade. She had learned most of the words to the "Ladies and Jellybeans" speech. She was up to "foursies" in jacks. Work was easy because Mrs. Boggs was just reviewing things they had learned the year before. And she had three for-sure friends, not just one or two.

At lunch, she sat with Regina and Kristy. Regina didn't like Kristy. "The poor kid," she would whisper to Wendy. Wendy always asked Kristy to sit with them. She knew how it felt to be left out.

During recess, she played with Nelson. The boys usually played kickball in the field, leaving the girls—and Nelson—to play games on the blacktop.

Wayne Supinger started calling Nelson "sissypants." Robert and the other boys copied everything Wayne did.

"I can play kickball," Nelson told Wendy wistfully. "I played soccer back in Germany. I'm a good kicker. But the guys won't let me. They don't like me."

"Why?" Wendy asked.

Nelson shrugged. "Because I'm different, I guess. I didn't come from here."

"You're not the only kid who isn't from

here," Wendy said. She was, but she knew a lot of kids at her school came from other places, like Nelson. Nelson had lived in Germany and the Philippines before that. His father was in the air force. Nelson's family lived in different places, wherever the air force sent Mr. Andrews.

"Wayne says I'm not an American. But I am!" Nelson said.

Wendy didn't think that not being an American was any reason not to like someone. She was glad to have Nelson as a friend. When they played jacks on the blacktop, he could scoop them all up in a single bounce.

For Wendy, life was almost perfect.

Then she found out something that made all her old worries seem like grains of sand. Suddenly she had a great big new worry. A *real* one.

It started when Denise came home from her Scout meeting feeling sick. The sickness wasn't anything to worry about. Denise often had colds and sore throats.

Once Wendy heard her mother say to a friend, "My oldest girl is sickly." Wendy was surprised. She thought *sickly* meant somebody like Charlotte Blevins, a fourth grader who rode Wendy's bus. Charlotte had polio and wore braces on both legs. Wendy wasn't sure what polio was, but she knew Charlotte couldn't walk without the braces. She bit her lip whenever she saw Charlotte struggle to climb the bus steps. Charlotte never wanted any help. Even though Denise had a lot of colds, Wendy thought, at least she could run and jump.

After supper that Friday of Denise's sickness, Wendy went with her mother to People's Drugstore to buy Denise some cough syrup. In the store Wendy was supposed to stay with Mrs. Fletcher, but somehow she strayed into the toy aisle.

The glossy cover of a book caught Wendy's eye. It was called *The Giant Book of Birds*. Eagerly she paged through it. The book about birds in the school library didn't have nearly so many pictures or such pretty ones. She *had* to have this book.

Holding it like a prize, she skipped over to the medicine section of the store. Her mother was reading the label on a bottle of cough syrup.

"Mama, see what I found!" she exclaimed. "Will you buy it for me?" She knew she shouldn't beg in stores, but she *loved* this book.

Mrs. Fletcher glanced at the book. A funny expression came over her face. "I'm sorry," she said. "You can't have the book."

"It's about birds. Look at the neat pictures. I could use it for school."

"I said I'm sorry, Wendy. The book costs five ninety-nine. I have enough money for Denise's medicine and that's all."

Wendy put the book back on the rack in the toy aisle. Maybe in a day or so her mother would change her mind. She wasn't the type to sulk and, anyway, she had high hopes that her mother would be in a better mood in a few days.

At home, Wendy helped Mrs. Fletcher dry the supper dishes. Usually Denise helped, but she was excused because she was sick. They could hear her coughing in her room on the other side of the kitchen.

"I think Denise should see the doctor tomorrow," Mrs. Fletcher said.

Mr. Fletcher put his newspaper down. He always read the newspaper after supper, sitting at the kitchen table. "The cough syrup you bought won't help?"

"It sounds like it's gone into her chest. Probably bronchitis again."

"Then take her in as soon as the medical center opens," Mr. Fletcher said. "I've got good insurance with this new job. The doctor bills will be taken care of."

Mrs. Fletcher sighed. "But we have so many other expenses. The new hot water heater, that tax bill in July—"

"No doubt about it, we're having a tight year," Mr. Fletcher said.

"What's a tight year?" Wendy asked. She pictured a calendar wound up with rubber bands.

Her father glanced at her. Obviously Mr. Fletcher had forgotten she was still there.

"Nothing for you to worry about," he said reassuringly.

Mrs. Fletcher handed Wendy a glass of bubbly ginger ale. "Here. Take this to Denise."

Wendy wished she could be sick and get to lie in bed and read comic books and have ginger ale with a bendy straw in the glass. When she went into Denise's room, she told her so.

"No you don't," Denise said, coughing. "It's no fun being sick. My medicine tastes awful. And before I go to sleep, Mama rubs my chest with Vicks VapoRub. Pee-yew! Does that stuff stink!"

"Denise," Wendy said, sitting on the edge of her bed. "Daddy said we're having a tight year. What does that mean? Daddy wouldn't tell me."

"It means we don't have much money. I think it's because Daddy changed jobs. He made more money at his old job but he gets better insurance and stuff at his new job."

"What's insurance?" Wendy asked.

"I don't know. I didn't hear that part."

Denise's bed was right against the wall. Wendy knew she could count on Denise overhearing all sorts of interesting things.

Now Wendy understood her mother's funny expression in the drugstore. People having a tight year did not spend money on bird books.

She thought about Kristy Bostic, who'd worn the same dress to school every day for two weeks. Kristy also got her lunch free. There were other free-lunch kids in Wendy's class. She knew if you couldn't pay for your lunch, you were poor. Wendy couldn't buy lunch, either, but she brought her lunch from home. She didn't know if that made her poor or not.

"Are we poor?" she asked Denise.

Denise sneezed. Reaching for a tissue, she replied, "I guess so. I hope I don't have to quit Girl Scouts."

"What if my feet grow and bust right through my old shoes? Mama said my shoes had to hold out till Christmas." Wendy imagined her toes sticking out of her shoes as she walked through the snow.

Mrs. Fletcher entered Denise's room, bringing the dreaded jar of Vicks VapoRub. "Wendy, you shouldn't be on Denise's bed. You might catch her cold."

Wendy slid off. "We were talking about being poor. Mama, will we have to get free lunches at school?"

Her mother set the jar on the nightstand. "Whatever gave you that idea? We are not poor. Money is just tight, that's all."

"Then I won't have to quit Girl Scouts?" Denise asked.

Mrs. Fletcher sighed. "Why are you girls worrying? Everything will be fine. We don't have money for extras—foolishness—but we have plenty for the necessities. Wendy, bedtime. Scoot."

In her own room, Wendy got out her red change purse from the bureau drawer. She counted the coins as they dropped one by one into her palm. Eleven pennies. Not nearly enough for *The Giant Book of Birds*.

Maybe her parents would need this money, she thought. Maybe she should save it in case they ran out of food. Eleven pennies would buy eleven pieces of Turkish taffy from George's store. At least they wouldn't starve.

Her mother came in to kiss her good-night.

"Mama," Wendy said. "Is a bird book foolishness or a necessity?"

Mrs. Fletcher smiled as she tucked the sheet under Wendy's chin. "Wendy, you don't need new toys to have fun. You can make your own fun, like my sisters and I used to do."

Wendy yawned. "Back in the olden days? What did you do?"

"Oh, we played games and made paper dolls out of old catalogs. Homemade fun. And it didn't cost a cent." She left the door open a crack so Wendy's room wouldn't be completely dark.

∎∎∎∎∎∎∎∎∎∎∎

The next day Denise's cold was worse. Mrs. Fletcher took her to the medical center. Denise was upset because she had to miss the special Scout trip to a farm. She even cried, and Denise hardly ever cried.

Wendy was upset because she knew Denise's sickness meant she might never get her bird book, not until the tight year was over.

While Denise and Mrs. Fletcher were gone, Wendy stayed home with her father. They worked outside, raking huge piles of leaves, which they heaped in a wheelbarrow. Then they rolled the wheelbarrow to the edge of the woods and dumped the leaves.

A blackbird flapped across the blue sky. Wendy tipped her head back to watch its flight. The bird reminded her again of the book in the drugstore. How could her mother think it was a toy? *The Giant Book of Birds* wasn't a toy—it was something she really *needed.* Maybe her father would understand.

"Daddy," Wendy asked. "Which is better, homemade fun or store-bought fun?"

Mr. Fletcher whisked the rake over the

lawn. "Oh, homemade fun, definitely."

That was not the answer she had hoped for. Wendy tried another approach. "Let's say you had two things you could do. Watch TV or read a book about birds. A special book with lots of pictures. It's called *The Giant Book of Birds*."

"I don't think watching television falls into the category of homemade fun," Mr. Fletcher said. The wheelbarrow billowed with the leaves he threw in it. "But that bird book sounds interesting. Did you get it at the library?"

Wendy shook her head sadly. "No, it's at the drugstore. It costs five ninety-nine. Mama says it's too expensive."

"Your mother worries about money too much."

"Then a book is a necessity?" Wendy said hopefully.

"Sounds like this one is. Too bad your mother has the car or we could drive there now. Hey, let's take the wheelbarrow!" With one quick motion, he swung Wendy up on top of the leaves. Lifting the handles, he began running.

"Daddy!" Wendy squealed.

He steered like a crazy person, winding in and out of trees, around in circles, back and forth across the yard. Wendy hung on to the metal sides, shrieking with laughter. This was more fun than the rides at the firemen's carnival! She laughed even harder when he dumped her out on the huge leaf pile next to the woods.

"Are we there? Are we at the store?" her father cried, with mock dismay. "Oh, no, we're still in our backyard!"

Wendy brushed leaves from her corduroy pants, giggling. "Daddy, you're so silly!" Then she climbed back in the wheel-barrow. "That was fun. Can we do it again?"

"Your poor old father is pooped," he said wearily. "But maybe I can push you to the house, if you promise to push me next time."

Mr. Fletcher rolled Wendy across the yard. The big front tire bumped over hills and ruts. Wendy's knees joggled up and down. She could smell crushed leaves lining the bottom of the wheelbarrow. It smelled like . . . fall! Fall must finally be here.

When they reached the porch, her father tilted the wheelbarrow so Wendy could tumble out. Then they raked the rest of the leaves.

▪▪▪▪▪▪▪▪▪▪▪

Denise came home feeling worse than ever. She and her mother had waited a long time to see the doctor, who said Denise had bronchitis and had to go straight to bed. Now Denise had new medicine that tasted even worse than the cough syrup. For the rest of the afternoon, Wendy stayed in her own room, coloring quietly, while her sister slept.

After supper, Mr. Fletcher went out for a while. He came back with a big paper sack.

"Knock, knock!" he called, stopping by Denise's door. "I have surprises for any interested kids. Do I hear any takers?"

Wendy flew into the hall. "Me! Me!"

"Me, too!" Denise croaked.

Wendy followed her father into Denise's room. He put the bag on the floor and began taking things out. Mrs. Fletcher came to the door to watch.

"How'd that get in my bag?" Mr.

Fletcher asked himself, frowning. "I thought I bought a screwdriver." He handed Denise a crossword puzzle book. "I don't suppose you'd want that, would you?"

Denise clutched the book to her chest. "You can't take it back now!" she said through her stuffed-up nose.

Then he pulled out a new *Uncle Scrooge* comic book, a package of cherry licorice whips, and three bottles of Zippy Fruit Punch, Denise's favorite soft drink. "The clerk must have put these in by mistake, too. Do you want them?"

Wendy watched with a heart growing heavier by the minute. She knew her sister deserved presents. After all, she was the sick one who had to miss her Scout trip. But wasn't Wendy an interested kid, too, even if she wasn't sick?

Now Mr. Fletcher was reaching way

down in the bag. "Something's stuck." He handed the bag to Wendy. "Your hands are small. Can you get it out?"

It was probably a ballerina wallet for Denise, Wendy thought. Her sister loved things decorated with ballerinas.

Wendy peered into the bag. There, at the very bottom, was—wonder of wonders!—the glossy *Giant Book of Birds*.

"One very necessary bird book," her mother said, smiling.

Wendy yelped with joy. "Daddy! My book! Oh, thank you! Mama, look! He got me my book. I won't ask for another thing this whole tight year, I promise." She hugged her precious book. She'd love it forever and ever.

Her father patted her on the head. "I told you girls not to worry. Especially you, Wendy. We might be having a tight year,

but we all need little treats now and then."
He left the girls alone.

Wendy watched her father stride down the hall. His work shoes squeaked a little. He worked so hard at his new job, late many evenings. Who gave him little treats?

Denise ripped open the package of licorice. "Want some?"

"In a minute," Wendy replied. "I have to do something."

Back in her bedroom, she fished the eleven pennies from her red purse. Then she tiptoed across the hall to her parents' room. Her father had a pewter dish on his dresser that he kept loose change in. He often let Wendy or Denise snitch a dime from the dish for a Popsicle.

Today the dish was empty. Wendy dropped her eleven pennies into the pewter bowl. Wouldn't her father be surprised! He needed little treats, too. He could buy himself a banana Popsicle and have enough left over for a piece of Turkish taffy.

Gazing out the window, she noticed the wheelbarrow propped against the porch. It'd been so much fun when her father pushed her around the yard. Maybe when Denise was better, they could give each other rides. Long rides, as long as they wanted.

And it wouldn't cost them a cent.

CHAPTER THREE

Learning a New Way

Wendy had been a third grader for nearly a month when she decided to give her teacher a present. She chose a morning when Mrs. Boggs was alone at her desk. She didn't want anyone to see her, afraid the other kids might make fun of her. Wayne liked to call kids names. He called Nelson "sissypants" and he called Sandra

"Goody Two Shoes" because she offered to erase the board for Mrs. Boggs.

Wendy approached Mrs. Boggs's desk shyly, her arm behind her back. "I brought you something," she whispered.

Mrs. Boggs smiled broadly. "A present! Wendy, how nice."

Wendy held out her hand. On her palm lay a smooth, creamy rock. "I found it in my driveway. It's almost perfectly round, except for this little bump on the end."

Mrs. Boggs gasped with pleasure. "What a beautiful stone! It'll make a wonderful paperweight." She set the stone on a stack of arithmetic papers. It rested on its oblong bottom, like an egg. Wendy thought the rock looked as if it had been made to hold down her teacher's papers.

"I'll treasure this always," Mrs. Boggs said. "Thank you, Wendy."

"You're welcome." Wendy beamed. Her teacher really liked it! She had worried that Mrs. Boggs would think it was just a dumb old rock. But she should have known her teacher would see it as a thing of beauty.

Wendy believed she and Mrs. Boggs had a special understanding. She would bring her teacher presents, and then Mrs. Boggs wouldn't call on her during class. Instead, they would talk in private, at Mrs. Boggs's desk.

Maybe she would bring another present tomorrow. A persimmon! Ripe persimmons hung heavily on the tree by her father's shed, golden and beautiful.

"I think it's time to start, don't you?" Mrs. Boggs said, gently reminding Wendy to sit down. She smiled the smile Wendy loved to see.

"Yes, Mrs. Boggs." She skipped back to

her seat. A smile swelled inside her until it tugged the corners of her mouth upward. She couldn't help it. She felt like smiling and smiling and smiling!

"What are you grinning at?" asked Nelson.

"Nothing," Wendy replied cheerfully. "It's just a smiley sort of day, don't you think?"

"I thought you were posing for a jack-o'-lantern or something."

Regina Coopersmith thought this was terribly funny. She didn't usually laugh at Nelson's jokes.

Wendy wasn't upset. She knew Nelson was her friend.

Once Nelson brought a set of chopsticks and a small blue-painted china cup from the Far East to Sharing. Wayne Supinger teased him about playing with girls and having tea parties. Wendy knew Nelson was her friend, but he also really wanted to fit in. Nelson made wisecracks so the other boys would think he was regular.

After the Pledge, Mrs. Boggs asked if anyone had something special to share. Regina got up to show the class a chinchilla fur muff. Wendy wondered when she would have anything nearly as nice to share. There was her new bird book. But even if she brought it to school, she'd be too scared to stand up in front of the class.

Then Mrs. Boggs asked each row to come up to her desk and get their cursive workbooks. Wendy went up with Regina and the others in her row. Her workbook was easy to spot; she had printed "Wendy F." under the title on the mottled green cover: *Learning a New Way*.

Last week, Mrs. Boggs had asked each

student to bring in $1.50 to pay for the workbooks. Wendy had worried that her parents might not have the money, but Mrs. Fletcher said that school supplies were a necessity. Wendy brought her dollar and two quarters in the very next day. So did Regina and Nelson. But Wendy noticed that Kristy stared at the floor all week whenever Mrs. Boggs asked if anyone had their workbook money.

Still, when the workbooks came, Mrs. Boggs had handed Kristy one, just like everyone else. Wendy overheard her teacher whisper to Kristy that she didn't have to worry about the money. She decided Mrs. Boggs must have paid for Kristy's workbook herself. That made Wendy love her third grade teacher all the more.

Now Wendy opened her workbook to the first page. They had to copy sentences in their best printing. A sort of farewell to their old way of writing. Wendy had made only one little mistake.

I saw a baby bir
d. It was flying.
I can read a book.
I have a raincoat.

Just looking at her almost-perfect sentences brought another smile to Wendy's face. Denise had given her a skinny yellow pencil, so she wouldn't have to write with a big fat baby pencil anymore. So far, cursive hadn't been much different from printing. In her workbook, Wendy had been making circles and sticks. She liked drawing circles and sticks.

"Okay, class," said Mrs. Boggs. "I want you to begin the exercise on page seven. Today we will learn how to make downstrokes. Strokes connect your letters in handwriting." She went to the blackboard and drew long, sweeping lines. "Slant your workbook and make the strokes about one finger apart."

Wendy glanced over at Nelson. He was drawing strokes rapidly. Nelson could already write cursive. Once he'd passed Wendy a note written in cursive and she'd had to ask him what it said. The school Nelson went to in Germany was ahead of what they were doing in Warrensville Elementary. Nelson could do fractions, too.

Biting her bottom lip, Wendy began drawing strokes. Right away she noticed hers were not like the ones in the workbook or the long, sweeping strokes Mrs. Boggs put on the blackboard. Wendy's strokes were wiggly. They were also too close together, like a bunch of frightened sheep.

She made the next row farther apart. These strokes were too far apart, like lone trees in a vast field.

Nelson watched her. "Don't be so stiff," he said. "You're not supposed to draw—it's writing."

"But that's the way I print," Wendy said, printing a perfect W.

She sneaked a peek at Kristy's work. The girl hunched over her workbook, the ends of her stringy hair brushing the page. She was slowly drawing her strokes, too, but they looked better than Wendy's. Probably, Wendy thought, she wanted to show Mrs. Boggs she hadn't wasted her money.

The teacher walked up and down the aisles, checking everyone's progress. She paused by Wendy's desk. Wendy gave her a special smile.

Mrs. Boggs didn't smile back. "Your undercurves are pretty good, Wendy. But you need to touch the top of the line when you make downcurves." Taking the pencil from Wendy's hand, she sketched four quick strokes. The bottom of the downcurve seemed to sprout from the thick line and the top stopped exactly on the line above.

"Now you try it," she said, handing Wendy back her pencil.

With her tongue between her teeth, Wendy made four wobbly downcurves. Her strokes still looked like lopsided candy canes.

"Don't hook so much at the top. You'll get the hang of it. Just keep at it." Mrs. Boggs patted Wendy on the back, then moved down the row to examine Regina's workbook. She clucked her tongue. "Oh, Regina. You can do better than that."

Wendy grinned to herself. Regina's work

was crummy, too. Knowing that one of her friends was having trouble with cursive made her feel better.

After they practiced making strokes for a while, Mrs. Boggs went to the board again. This time she drew a swooping shape on the blackboard.

"A capital *D*," she said. "This is the heel and this is the toe." With her chalk, she pointed to loops at the bottom of the letter. "Don't let the heel or toe of your *D* fall beneath the line," she warned.

"Oooh, that looks hard," Regina whispered to Wendy.

"I know," Wendy agreed. "I'll never be able to do it."

"Me either."

"I'll probably mess up," Wendy said cheerfully. She decided that she liked Regina a lot, maybe even better than Nelson and Kristy. She and Regina had something in common.

Mrs. Boggs wasn't finished. She added a lowercase *d* beside the big *D*. "The strokes you learned today are used in these letters. Slant your book toward the right. Let's finish the exercise on page eight. Watch those heels and toes!"

They began practicing big *D*'s and little *d*'s. Wendy didn't try to make hers very good. She knew Regina's would be just as bad as hers. Mrs. Boggs wouldn't scold her without scolding Regina, too. Wendy doubted Mrs. Boggs would scold them at all.

She looked around her. Nelson had finished the exercise. He was sketching a rocket ship zooming through space.

Wendy checked out Kristy's workbook. Kristy's letters weren't perfect like Nelson's, but she was still a better cursive-writer than Wendy.

Wendy tapped Regina on the shoulder. "Are you done yet? Wasn't it awful?"

Regina made a swatting gesture. "Don't bother me. I think I'm getting the hang of it."

Panic-stricken, Wendy knelt in her seat to look over Regina's shoulder. Neat rows of big *D*'s and little *d*'s marched across her workbook page. Regina had learned how to write cursive! How could she do this to Wendy, her own friend? They were supposed to be terrible in cursive together!

Wendy glanced around the classroom. Everyone was bent over his or her workbook. Robert and Kristy and Nelson, they were all writing. Even Wayne, who didn't like to do anything the teacher asked him to do. Even Sandra, who was only seven!

"Okay," Mrs. Boggs said after a while. "Turn the page. I'd like you to try the practice sentence. I know there are strokes we haven't covered yet, but you've mastered most of them by now."

Wendy's heart sank when she read over the sentence Mrs. Boggs wanted them to copy: "Did you ever see the Little Dipper in a dark December sky?" It was loaded with big *D*'s and little *d*'s. And it was *all* in cursive!

Bending low over her workbook, Wendy began writing. Her big *D*'s were terrible. The heel and toe came below the line. She erased the capital *D* in "Did." This time she tried to keep the first loop, the part Mrs. Boggs called the toe, on the line. But the heel, which came right after the toe, dropped way below the line.

At the end of the fourth line, Wendy realized she'd started her sentence over too far. It read "Did you ever see the Little Dip" before running off the page.

She felt like crying. At the rate she was going, she'd never have any best work to put in her Birdland file folder. Cursive was impossible!

A shadow crossed Wendy's desk. Mrs. Boggs leaned over her workbook, noting the messy *D*'s.

"Having trouble, Wendy?" the teacher inquired in her gentle voice.

"I ran out of room," Wendy explained lamely. "We only have four measly lines. We had more lines in our old workbooks."

"That was for printing," Mrs. Boggs said. "When you print, you need more space. With cursive, you'll be able to write the same words in less space. You'll save paper."

"Do we *have* to learn cursive?"

Wendy's teacher smiled, showing a dimple. "Yes, Wendy, you have to learn cursive. You don't want to print forever, do you?" She turned away to look at Kristy's workbook.

Yes, she *did* want to print forever. In printing, you didn't have any of that heel and toe stuff. You just made circles and sticks and put them together.

"Printing is for babies," Nelson declared.

"So?" Wendy said grumpily.

"What if you want to buy a car? You go to the car lot and pick out a car. And then the man hands you a contract to sign. How would it look if you printed your name in big letters at the bottom? The man would think you couldn't even drive."

"I can't drive," Wendy said. "And I can't make *D*'s, either."

"It's not hard, Wendy," said Kristy. "Just pretend you're ice-skating. Only on paper."

Wendy couldn't ice-skate on ice, much less on paper. She frowned. Her friends thought they were so smart, writing cursive. If they were *really* her friends, they wouldn't make her feel bad.

Mrs. Boggs reviewed Regina's work. "Very good," she praised. The teacher held up Regina's workbook so the entire class could see the neat *D*'s.

Regina swung around to grin at Wendy. "My page is the best in the whole room."

"So what?" Wendy said sourly. She didn't like Regina nearly as much as she did a few minutes ago. In fact, she didn't like any of her friends very much. Let them write their dumb old cursive and get good grades.

The bell rang for lunch. As Wendy passed her desk, Mrs. Boggs set the smooth cream-colored rock on the stack of workbooks.

"Your present certainly comes in handy," she told Wendy.

Wendy didn't reply. She didn't like her teacher, either, as much as she did that morning. Mrs. Boggs would probably send her back to her old second grade class. "Printers belong in second grade," she'd say.

No doubt about it, Wendy thought, cursive would be her downfall. She didn't stand a chance.

CHAPTER FOUR

Bombs from the Sky

On October first, Wendy's mother let her change the calendar in the kitchen. The new picture showed a field of pumpkins.

"Time goes by so fast," Mrs. Fletcher remarked.

Wendy didn't think time was going by fast at all. Every day that she couldn't learn cursive felt like a year.

"I need to borrow the newspaper for school," Denise said, sniffling. "Okay?"

"Bring it back so your father can read it tonight," Mrs. Fletcher said. "Are you coming down with another cold?"

"No. My nose is just running." Denise grabbed the newspaper and her lunch and rushed out the door first, as usual.

Wendy hurried after her. At the bus stop, Denise skimmed the newspaper headlines for current events. Wendy glimpsed familiar words in the headline: RUSSIA and COLD WAR. She'd heard those words on the news her father watched on TV every night. And those words were often in the paper, in big letters.

This morning, the school bus was late.

Wendy was tired of waiting, tired of watching Denise read the newspaper. Even though it was the start of a brand-new month, it seemed like an ordinary Monday.

Denise wasn't paying attention to her, so Wendy began to climb the bank beside their driveway. The bank rose like a small mountain. It was covered with brambles that snagged Wendy's skirt. "Beggar's lice," triangular-shaped burrs, clung to her socks.

At the top of the bank was a highway marker. At least, that's what Mr. Fletcher said it was. But Wendy had it in her head that the marker was a stone a pirate had put there to mark buried treasure. Today she'd love to find the pirate's treasure, gold coins and ruby necklaces. Then her family wouldn't have a tight year anymore.

Wendy struggled up the steep hillside. Pulling vines away, she uncovered a square cement post sunk in the ground. Covered with dirt, number 1675 was stamped in the middle.

Would a pirate use a cement post to mark his treasure? she wondered. Probably not. Maybe it was an old highway marker after all.

Sighing, Wendy climbed down the bank. A flash of blue in the grass made her stop. Reaching into the weeds, she plucked out a blue feather. A blue jay wing feather! There was a picture of a feather just like this in her *Giant Book of Birds*.

Maybe . . . the thought grew in Wendy's mind. Yes, she *could* take the feather to Sharing. It was so pretty that she forgot, for the moment, to worry about getting up in front of class.

"Bus!" Denise yelled, waving her newspaper.

All the way to school, Wendy had to pick other burrs, sticklike "hitchhikers," off her skirt, but she was happy. At last she had something to share, something that would surely fascinate everyone, even Wayne Supinger.

IIIIIIIIIII

The first thing Wendy noticed that was different in Room 5 was the noise. Mrs. Boggs was in the office. Wendy had seen her there when she passed the glass windows. She knew her teacher would not be pleased if she heard all the racket.

The noise was coming from the kids crowded around Regina Coopersmith. They were laughing and talking excitedly about a silvery, furry animal in Regina's arms. That was the second different thing. The animal looked sort of like a rabbit, only without long ears. Wendy knew at once it was Regina's pet chinchilla, Fluffy.

Dismayed, Wendy tugged her feather from her notebook. A feather was dumb compared to a real live chinchilla. How could Regina do this to her? Wendy threw the feather in the wastebasket next to Mrs. Boggs's desk, then sat down at her own. She took out her spelling words and began to study them. Let the others squeal and carry on over a fuzzy animal. *She* had more important things to do.

Finally, Mrs. Boggs came in and clapped her hands. "Okay, class. Quiet, please. In your seats. Regina, put Fluffy in his cage. We'll have Sharing after the roll."

"He'll stay in my lap," Regina told the teacher. "He won't bother anybody." She cuddled the chinchilla as she sat down at her desk.

Kristy watched Fluffy explore the folds of Regina's jumper, then leaned across the aisle. "He's the cutest thing I've ever seen. I wish I could hold him."

"I might let you hold him," Regina said loftily. Bringing a real live animal to school had given her enormous power. Wendy liked Regina less by the minute. It was bad enough she had to go and learn cursive, but now she was Queen of Sharing.

After Mrs. Boggs called the roll and they recited the Pledge, she said, "All right, Regina. You may bring Fluffy up."

Regina carried her chinchilla to the front of the room. She set Fluffy on the table and began talking. She told the class about Fluffy's special fur and how he liked to chew paper. Wendy was envious of the way Regina talked in front of the whole class. She wasn't afraid of anything.

Then Regina strolled between the rows so each student could pet Fluffy. When she paused by Wendy's desk, Wendy pretended to be studying her spelling.

"Don't you want to pet him?" Regina asked.

Wendy shook her head. "No, thanks. I don't pet strange animals."

"Fluffy isn't strange!" Regina said indignantly. "He's my pet!"

Kristy eagerly touched the chinchilla, burying her fingers in his dense fur with an exclamation of delight. Even Nelson stroked Fluffy. Wendy was the only person in Room 5 who didn't pet Regina's chinchilla.

"Thank you very much for sharing Fluffy with us," Mrs. Boggs said to Regina. "You may put him in his cage now."

Regina unlatched the door of a wire cage and gently pushed Fluffy inside. The chinchilla immediately settled in a nest of paper and rags. Regina placed the cage importantly by her desk, next to Wendy.

Wendy moved her spelling list to the corner of her desk so she wouldn't have to stare at Regina's dumb old chinchilla. Just as she was deciding she didn't want Regina for a friend, there was a knock at the classroom door. A big boy handed Mrs. Boggs a note. The teacher read it, then cleared her throat, like she did before important announcements.

"We are going to start having air raid drills," she said. "Our first one will be at ten o'clock."

"An air raid drill!" Nelson cried.

"When the siren goes off," Mrs. Boggs explained, "we will line up and leave the room in an orderly manner. Absolutely no running and no talking. I'll tell you what to do when we get out in the hall."

The other kids started talking, as if this were going to be fun. But Wendy noticed how serious her teacher looked. A new worry gnawed at her stomach. Why were they having air raid drills? What did it mean?

At exactly ten o'clock a swoopy siren went off, a chilling sound unlike the familiar firehouse whistle. The class filed out of the room. Other classes milled in the hall. Mrs. Boggs led her students to the wall nearest their door.

"Kneel down," she instructed them. "Pretend you are a turtle. Scrunch up so you take up as little space as possible. Put your head down on the floor. Then clasp your hands behind your neck. Here, Regina will show you."

Always Regina! Wendy thought.

Regina scrunched up like a turtle. Mrs. Boggs gently pushed Regina's neck down until her forehead was resting on the floor.

Regina laced her fingers behind her neck.

"All right, class," Mrs. Boggs said. "Let's see how quickly and quietly we can get into this position. Wayne, no fooling around."

Wendy was in line behind Nelson and in front of Kristy. She tucked her knees under her body and laid her forehead on the cool tile floor.

"Closer together," Mrs. Boggs ordered. "We need to make room for everyone. There shouldn't be more than an inch between you and your neighbor."

Everyone scooched forward. Nelson's feet were practically touching Wendy's head. She could see the scratches in the soles of his shoes. A chunk of gravel was stuck in one heel.

"Head down, Wendy," Mrs. Boggs said. She pushed Wendy's head down and brought her hands up to fit around the back of her neck. "Clasp your fingers together. You have to protect your neck. Good, Nelson," she said, moving on.

"How long do we have to do this?" Nelson's voice was muffled.

"Until we hear the all-clear signal," the teacher replied. "No talking, please."

Wendy's head hurt from the hard floor and her legs were getting cramped. The tile smelled like sawdust and chalk. Across from her, Miss Stuart's fifth graders squatted in similar positions. Wendy wondered where Denise was. The sixth grade classes were upstairs.

The siren swooped on and on, sometimes louder, sometimes fainter. Nelson shifted his feet, catching a piece of Wendy's bangs. His shoes made funny scritching noises.

Wendy worried that her own shoes were bothering Kristy. She felt terrible sticking her shoes in somebody's face. To take her mind off her numb legs, she counted breaths.

At last the siren faded, then stopped altogether. Wendy lifted her head. A *beep-beep* issued from the PA system. The all-clear signal? Mrs. Boggs was getting up. She had been pretending to be a turtle, too.

"You may rise," she told her class.

Wendy thought her legs would buckle, but she managed to get to her feet. Everyone began chattering and laughing.

Nelson turned to grin at her. His face was red. "Hope my feet didn't smell too bad."

Wendy grinned back. She felt so relieved now that the siren was silent. "Pee-yew! Change your socks!" she said, pinching her nose with her fingers.

After Mrs. Boggs herded her class back

inside their room, nobody wanted to sit down. They were too excited.

Nelson knew all about air raid drills because of his father's job.

"Planes drop bombs from the sky," he explained. Wayne Supinger made a loud exploding noise.

"They drop bombs on schools?" Wendy asked nervously.

"I don't think they mean to hit schools and houses," Nelson said. "I guess they miss their targets sometimes."

Houses! Wendy hadn't thought about her house. Suppose a plane was getting ready to drop a bomb on her house right this second! "Who would want to drop a bomb on us?" she asked.

Suddenly Regina screamed. Wendy jumped, thinking a bomb had dropped.

Mrs. Boggs ran to Regina. "What is it?"

"Fluffy!" Regina wailed. "He's gone!"

Sure enough, the cage door stood open and Regina's chinchilla was nowhere to be seen.

"Oh, dear," Mrs. Boggs said. "How did that cage get open? Didn't you latch it firmly, Regina?"

Regina was bawling. "Fluffy ran away!" she sobbed.

"The drill probably frightened him. Don't worry, dear. We'll find him," Mrs. Boggs reassured her. "Everybody spread out," she commanded the class. "Look behind the registers, in the coat closet, in the desks."

Everyone began hunting for the lost chinchilla. Except Wendy. She didn't join in the search. She thought it served Regina right. It was only what she deserved, bringing a live animal to school.

Regina was crying too hard to hunt for her chinchilla. She looked as if she had lost her best friend. Wendy suddenly realized Regina loved her pet very much.

The class looked in every corner and behind all the furniture. But no Fluffy.

"I suppose he could have run out into the hall," Mrs. Boggs said. "We had our heads down, so we wouldn't have seen him. Let's go, class."

Everyone but Wendy hurried out into the hall. Regina followed, still sobbing. It seemed Fluffy was really gone.

Wendy stood alone in the deserted classroom. Poor Regina! She knew how terrible it felt to lose a friend. After all, she had lost Debbie. Then Wendy remembered how she hadn't wanted Regina for a friend anymore, just because she'd brought Fluffy to school. That seemed pretty silly now.

Wendy wished she could make her friend happy again. If she were a chinchilla, where would she go? Especially during an air raid drill?

I'd want to get away from the noise, Wendy thought. Someplace safe . . .

What would be a good hiding place for a scared chinchilla? She remembered how Fluffy made a nest in the pile of rags and papers.

Wendy sprinted over to Mrs. Boggs's desk. She peeped into the wastepaper basket. Sure enough, a ball of silvery fur lay dozing in a nest of chewed paper. Fluffy!

At that moment, Regina came into the room. Her nose was running. She snatched a tissue from the box Mrs. Boggs kept on her desk.

"I found him!" Wendy cried. "He's in here, safe and sound."

"Fluffy!" Regina ran over and lifted the chinchilla from the can. She kissed his head. "Oh, Fluffy! You're all right! Don't ever run away again." She smiled through her tears at Wendy. "Thanks. That was pretty smart, looking in the trashcan. Nobody else thought of it."

"I just figured he'd want to hide in some paper," Wendy said modestly.

"Do you want to hold him? He's not a strange animal anymore. You saved his life."

Wendy took the chinchilla. Fluffy's fur was kitten soft and his little heart beat thumpity-thump. She stroked him a minute, then handed him back to Regina.

"I think he's still scared."

Regina put him in his cage and latched the door carefully. "I shouldn't have brought him. My mother said he'd be scared."

"I'm glad you did," Wendy said, surprising herself. "Fluffy is a nice pet."

"He's my best friend. I mean, not counting my real friends. You and Kristy and Nelson." Regina laughed. "Even though Nelson is a know-it-all!"

They could hear the others coming down the hall. Somebody, probably Wayne Supinger, was imitating an air raid siren.

"You know, I was really scared when that siren went off," Regina admitted.

Wendy couldn't believe it! Regina never acted afraid of anything. She could stand up in front of the whole class and talk a blue streak.

"I was, too," Wendy said. "I don't understand why anyone would want to drop a bomb on us."

"I don't either," Regina agreed. They looked at each other. Air raid drills remained a mystery, but one thing was certain—they were friends, real friends, because they had been afraid together.

■■■■■■■■■■■

On the bus ride home, Wendy asked her sister about the air raid drill.

"Who would drop a bomb on us?" she asked. She had been asking that question all day, it seemed.

Denise had the answer. "The Russians. They have these rockets that carry bombs. If the Russians set off the rockets, the bombs will fall on Washington, because that's where President Eisenhower lives. Washington isn't very far from Warrensville, you know. That's why we have to hide in the halls."

Wendy still had a hard time understanding why she had to pretend to be a turtle because some Russians had built rockets.

"Are the Russians mad at us? What did we ever do to them?"

"I don't know exactly," Denise said. "I think it's because we're different from them."

Wendy didn't even know any Russian people. She shivered, the way she did when the sun suddenly ducked under a cloud.

"Don't worry," Denise told her. "The president is trying his hardest to keep the bombs away from us."

Wendy wanted to believe her sister. She really did. But she kept remembering the rapid thumpity-thump of Fluffy's heart as she held him. Even though she held him as gently as she could, Fluffy was still afraid.

And so was she.

CHAPTER FIVE

The Wonder Bread Factory

During the next two weeks, there was an air raid drill at school almost every day. Wendy began to flinch whenever she heard a plane overhead. She was glad when she was absent for a few days with a cold. Then when Wendy returned, Mrs. Boggs told her class something that made Wendy put bombs in the back of her mind.

That Friday afternoon Wendy jumped excitedly on the bus. In her hand she clutched a permission slip. Denise was at her regular Scout meeting, and she was bursting to tell someone her news.

"Guess what?" Wendy said to the driver. "We're going on our field trip Monday!" All her life, it seemed, she had been waiting to go on the third grade class trip.

In first grade she went to the zoo. Last year she rode a train from Union Station to Alexandria. Next year, in fourth grade, she would visit Mount Vernon. But third graders—the luckiest ones in the whole school—got to go to the Wonder Bread factory!

When Denise went on her third grade class trip, she came home full of stories about the big machines that made bread and Twinkies and hot dog rolls. She described the wonderful yeasty smell of bread baking. Best of all was the miniature loaf of bread given to each child as a souvenir.

Denise had set her tiny loaf on the table for everyone to admire during supper.

Envious, Wendy had noticed that the little loaf of bread was perfect in every detail, right down to the red, blue, and yellow dots on the wrapper. For an entire week, Denise had fixed herself tiny peanut butter and jelly sandwiches, which she ate in two bites. She had little slices of buttered toast to go with her breakfast egg. Wendy longed to make peanut butter sandwiches no bigger than a matchbook cover.

Now *she* would visit the Wonder Bread factory in three more days.

When the bus stopped at her house, Wendy ran up the driveway and in the front door. Her mother was in the kitchen.

"Will you sign this?" Wendy asked, giving her mother the sweaty permission form. "We're going to the Wonder Bread factory Monday!"

"Field trip time already?" Mrs. Fletcher wiped her hands on a tea towel. "They don't give you much notice."

"Mrs. Boggs gave out the slips on Tuesday, but I wasn't there."

Then she remembered the field trip fee. "I also need a dollar," she said. The dollar part had worried Wendy all day. "Is that okay?"

"Of course," her mother assured her.

"Mrs. Boggs said we only need to bring a sandwich for lunch," she went on happily. "We're going to have free sodas and cupcakes at the Wonder Bread factory."

"What kind of sandwich would you like?"

"Anything," Wendy chirped. Who

needed a sandwich when there would be free cupcakes and sodas?

When Denise came home later from her Scout meeting, Wendy followed her into her room. "Guess what," she said. "We're going to the Wonder Bread factory Monday."

"So what?" Denise answered without enthusiasm. "I guess it's a big deal to little kids."

"I'll bet it's better than what the sixth graders do!" Wendy felt compelled to defend her field trip. Sometimes her sister acted so superior!

"We're going to Richmond in April," Denise said, kicking off her shoes. "Overnight. Mr. Hite is getting motel rooms for us."

"Well, we'll be gone the whole day," Wendy countered. It was hard to beat an overnight trip to Richmond. "We won't have to do any work."

"I bet my trip will cost a lot of money," Denise said thoughtfully. "I hope Mama will have enough."

"*My* trip only costs a dollar." Wendy was glad she could beat Denise on one point, at least. "And we get free cupcakes and sodas *and* a tiny loaf of bread to take home."

Denise unrolled her green knee socks. "Oh, yeah. I forgot about that little loaf of bread."

Wendy couldn't imagine forgetting such an important thing. Why, she'd remember her trip to the Wonder Bread factory her whole life.

▪▪▪▪▪▪▪▪▪▪▪▪

Field trip morning, Wendy sprang out of bed and put on her blue corduroy jumper. When she got to the kitchen, breakfast was already on the table. She quickly gobbled her cereal. On today of all days, she didn't want to be late for the bus.

While Wendy ate, Mrs. Fletcher fixed the girls' lunches. "Just a sandwich for me," Wendy reminded her.

"Is cheese okay?" her mother asked. "I used all the tuna fish for Denise's lunch."

Wendy hated cheese. But it didn't matter. She'd have lots of free cupcakes. "Cheese is okay," she told her mother. She printed "Wendy F." on the paper lunch bag her mother handed her.

With her dollar and her permission slip safely in her jumper pocket, Wendy skipped ahead of Denise down the driveway. She could hardly wait to get to school!

■■■■■■■■■■■

Room 5 was noisy. Everyone was talking and laughing. Mrs. Boggs flicked the lights on and off three times before the class settled down.

"In your seats," she ordered. "We have to collect permission slips and bus fares before we leave. Sandra's row looks ready. Let's start with them."

The row next to Wendy's filed up to Mrs. Boggs's desk. Kristy did not join the line. She sat at her desk, staring at her clasped hands.

"Aren't you going?" Wendy asked her.

Kristy shook her head. "I forgot to get my slip signed."

Wendy couldn't believe it! How could Kristy forget the field trip?

Mrs. Boggs saw her sitting there and came back to Kristy's desk. "Did you forget your dollar, Kristy?" she asked gently. "I'll loan it to you. You can pay me back whenever you can."

Kristy's blue eyes misted with tears. "I didn't have my slip signed," she whispered. "I forgot."

Mrs. Boggs patted her shoulder. "Oh, dear. You can't go without your mother's written permission. I'm so sorry."

Kristy wiped her eyes. "It's okay. I'll stay here. I didn't want to go anyway," she added bravely.

Everyone stared at Kristy, the only one in class who couldn't go on the trip.

Wendy felt sorry for her. If Kristy's family had only enough money for one dress for Kristy, did they have an extra dollar for her bus fare? Maybe Kristy just told Mrs. Boggs she forgot to have her slip signed.

A palm whacked Wendy's desk. "It's our turn," Regina said.

As Wendy got in line behind Regina, she saw Kristy's tearstreaked face beneath her curtain of hair. Wendy imagined her staying behind in Room 5 all by herself.

"Wake up." Regina jabbed Wendy in the ribs.

Wendy fished the dollar from her jumper pocket and gave it to Mrs. Boggs. But her permission slip wasn't there! She dug deeper, then she checked the other pocket.

"Wendy," Mrs. Boggs said. "We have to leave in a few minutes."

"I can't find my slip!" she wailed, turning her pockets inside out. "My mother signed it! Honest, she did! It fell out of my pocket!"

"Oh, that's too bad," Mrs. Boggs said sympathetically. "Look around your desk, dear. Maybe you dropped it on the floor."

Nelson helped her look. They found a drawing of Birdland and a red crayon Wendy thought she had lost, but no permission slip.

Wendy choked back tears. "Can you call my mother?" she asked Mrs. Boggs. "She'll tell you she signed it."

Her teacher shook her head sadly. "I must have her permission in writing. It's a school rule, Wendy."

"But she signed it! I just lost it!"

"I'm so sorry," Mrs. Boggs said. "You'll have to stay behind with Kristy. Wait a minute, please." She left the room. A moment later, she came back and said, "Wendy and Kristy? Come up here, please. Bring your things."

Wendy grabbed her lunch and crayons. Had Mrs. Boggs figured out a way for them to go on the trip, too? Maybe she was going to smuggle them on the bus. . . .

"I have arranged for you to stay in Miss Stuart's room while we are gone," Mrs. Boggs told them.

Wendy gulped. She and Kristy weren't going and they weren't staying in Room 5. They were being sent to a fifth grade class! How could they do fifth grade work? Wendy couldn't even write cursive yet.

Mrs. Boggs handed them each some mimeographs. "You won't be expected to do Miss Stuart's classwork, of course. Here are a few worksheets and some pictures for you to color. You may go now, girls. I'll see you when the class returns."

Worksheets! Wendy had planned to have the day off from work. Slowly she followed Kristy across the hall.

Miss Stuart waved them inside.

On shaking legs, Wendy entered the fifth grade room. Big kids gawked at them. A couple of girls giggled. Wendy crossed one foot over the other, the way she did when she was nervous. She felt very small.

97

Miss Stuart frowned at her class. "You know that two of Mrs. Boggs's students are spending the day with us. They are not Martians. There is no need to stare holes through them." She pointed to a pair of empty desks at the back of the room. "Wendy and Kristy, you may take those seats. If there is anything you need, let me know."

Wendy chose the desk closest to the window. It was too big, like everything else in the room. Her feet did not touch the floor. She put her lunch in the cubby under the desk and arranged her crayons on the too-high desk top.

Kristy sat across from her, with her chin on her fist.

Wendy shuffled through the worksheets. Work on a field trip day! At least they didn't have to do exercises in their cursive workbooks. Mrs. Boggs wanted them to sign their names in cursive now. But Wendy couldn't make the difficult capital W or the fancy F in her name.

It was very quiet in Miss Stuart's room. The fifth graders began working on decimals. Wendy could tell they were thinking hard. She wondered if she would be able to think that hard when she was a fifth grader.

At lunchtime, Wendy and Kristy walked down to the cafeteria with Miss Stuart's class. Fifth graders streamed into the lunchroom. The sixth graders were already taking seats.

While Kristy went to stand in line for her free-lunch tray, Wendy ducked behind a big boy. She didn't want her sister to see her. Denise would want to know why Wendy hadn't gone with her class to the

Wonder Bread factory. She'd tease her about losing her permission slip. Especially after she had tried to make her field trip sound so much better.

Denise sat down with a group of girls. She never noticed her sister among the taller fifth graders.

Wendy shook her lunch bag, miserably remembering the plain cheese sandwich her mother had packed. She still had her dollar. She could buy her lunch. Today they were having meat loaf. It smelled good.

But she would feel funny, she decided, paying money for her lunch when Kristy had to give the cafeteria lady a paper ticket. Maybe she could buy chocolate milk and an ice cream to go with her sandwich. Kristy wasn't allowed to buy chocolate milk or ice cream with her free-lunch ticket. Only regular food. Wendy didn't want to make her friend feel bad. She bought plain milk and that was all.

At the table, Wendy unwrapped her cheese sandwich. She wrinkled her nose. How she hated cheese!

Kristy's plate overflowed with meat loaf and lima beans and mashed potatoes. She stared at Wendy's lunch. "Is that all you have?" she asked.

Wendy nodded.

"I have a lot of food," Kristy said. "Do you like meat loaf? You can have half."

Wendy's mouth watered. "I don't have a plate. Or any silverware."

"Let's use your sandwich." Kristy cut half the meat loaf, which she placed on Wendy's sandwich. Then she added mashed potatoes and sprinkled half the lima beans on top.

Wendy laughed. "Hey! A cheese sandwich plate! Thanks."

"You can have my spoon to eat with," Kristy offered.

The girls giggled the whole lunch period. Kristy wasn't as shy when she was with Wendy. In fact, she was very funny.

After lunch they went outside for recess. The big kids played softball, but Wendy and Kristy were too small to join in. They sat on the swings at the end of the softball field and talked. When recess was over, they returned to Miss Stuart's classroom.

The afternoon dragged. Wendy colored pictures until her coloring hand ached. She saw that Kristy's crayons were broken, with the papers raggedly peeled. They lay on Kristy's desk unused. Crayons without papers always felt icky to Wendy. She didn't blame Kristy for not wanting to draw with such pathetic crayons.

"I'm tired of coloring," she said. "Want

to borrow my crayons for a while? I'm going to do the worksheets."

"Okay." Kristy took Wendy's crayons and eagerly began to color.

Wendy did half a worksheet, then stared forlornly out the window. Their class should be getting back soon. She bet they had a great time. And they would each have a tiny loaf of Wonder Bread. Wendy put her head down on her desk. Except for lunch, it had been a terrible day.

She must have dozed. Miss Stuart woke her up.

"You girls were so quiet, I forgot all about you," Miss Stuart said, smiling. "Pack your things. Your class is back."

Mrs. Boggs came to the fifth grade room to get them. Wendy ran to the door. She felt like crying, she was so glad to see her teacher.

"Miss Stuart tells me you two were great. I knew you would be. I can always count on Wendy and Kristy," Mrs. Boggs praised.

Wendy beamed at Kristy. She remembered again how much she liked their teacher.

Then Mrs. Boggs gave them each a tiny loaf of Wonder Bread, just like the big loaves, right down to the red, blue, and yellow dots on the wrapper.

Kristy marveled at the miniature perfection of the bread.

"You can make little-bitty peanut butter sandwiches," Wendy told her. "And eat them in two bites."

"Hey, I'll bring you a sandwich tomorrow," Kristy said. "We'll sit together at lunch, like today, okay?"

Wendy grinned through her tears. She could tell it made Kristy feel good to do something nice for her. Just because Kristy was poor, it didn't mean she couldn't share. Kristy was a real friend. Maybe it was worth missing the field trip to find that out.

CHAPTER SIX

Vaccination Clinic

The last day of October promised lots of excitement. That morning, Room 5 cut out paper jack-o'-lanterns to tape to the windows. Later that afternoon, the class would have a Halloween party, with cupcakes and Kool-Aid.

And during recess, Wendy discovered a new way to swing. When she and Nelson ran down the hill to the swing set, they found that the big kids had left the swings with the chains hitched up. The seats were too high to sit on, so Wendy suggested they drape themselves over the seats, lifting their feet.

Nobody else was around. The boys in their class were playing kickball. And the girls were jumping rope up on the blacktop.

"This was a good idea," Nelson said. His face was pink from hanging his head down as he swung.

Wendy let her swing carry her in a half-circle. "I like the swings best," she said. "I don't like the seesaw. It scares me when it flies up in the air. And I hate the bump when it comes down."

"I don't like the jungle gym," Nelson admitted in turn. "It hurts my hands to go across the monkey bars."

That was one nice thing about being friends with Nelson. He didn't make fun of her worries.

Wendy dragged the toe of her shoe in the dust beneath the swing. Then she remembered her shoes had to last almost two more months, until Christmas. It wasn't even Thanksgiving yet.

Just then Nelson stood up. His swing clipped him in the chest, but he didn't pay any attention.

"What is it?" Wendy asked, alarmed. She got off her swing, too.

Nelson didn't answer. He was staring in the direction of the parking lot next to the school. A blue van had pulled up by the front door.

A man in a suit and a woman in a blue dress walked into the school. Wendy recognized the light blue uniform of the county nurse. She guessed the man was the doctor who was supposed to come today.

The doctor was going to give everyone in Warrensville Elementary polio booster shots. Even the teachers. Even the principal.

Wendy had been anxious about getting the shot ever since Mrs. Boggs sent home the letter about the vaccination clinic. Last night she had tossed and turned in bed. Whenever she closed her eyes, she saw a giant needle coming right at her.

Nelson didn't know she was worried sick about the polio shot. Needles scared her a lot more than seesaws.

"Who are they?" Nelson asked.

"I think it's the doctor and the nurse," Wendy replied, trying to act cool about it.

"The shot doctor?" Nelson's eyes grew very wide. His face drained of color.

"Yes. You look awful," Wendy said. "Are you scared to get your shot?" She almost said, "Are you scared, too?"

"No—yes! Don't tell anybody, please," he begged. "I had a million shots when we went overseas. And they hurt. I just can't stand needles."

Nelson was scared, too. But he was actually trembling with fear. Wendy had never seen anyone so frightened in her life.

The bell rang. Recess was over. Mrs. Boggs's class lined up on the blacktop.

"All right, people," Mrs. Boggs said when everyone was present. "Remember last week we talked about vaccinations? The booster shots we need to keep us from getting polio."

Wendy thought about Charlotte Blevins, the fourth grader who had polio. She didn't want braces on her legs like Charlotte.

"We're going down to the auditorium now," Mrs. Boggs was saying. "The school has set up a clinic there and we will all get our polio boosters. Even me. I'll go first," she added, smiling.

Some of the kids became pale, like Nelson. A few started sniffling, as if they were going to cry.

"I don't want to go!" Wayne Supinger yelled as Mrs. Boggs led them down the hall.

"I'll stay with you the whole time," Mrs. Boggs reassured them.

"Will it hurt?" asked Regina.

"Only for a second," the teacher promised. "But you're all big boys and girls. Let's show the little children there's no reason to make a fuss."

They entered the auditorium where many classes had already gathered. First and second graders waited in line. Every one of them was bawling. Wendy felt like crying herself.

In front of the stage, a table had been set up. The doctor was shooting liquid into a needle. The nurse rubbed the arm of a sixth grade girl with a cotton ball. Then the doctor jabbed the needle into the girl's arm, releasing her with a smile. After the nurse taped a Band-Aid to her arm, the girl went up the other aisle and out of the auditorium. It was over so fast.

Wendy saw Denise's green Scout uniform near the front of the line. She waited until her sister glanced in her direction, then waved. Denise waved back.

"I'm going to faint," Nelson said in a weak voice. "I just know I'm going to faint."

"No, you aren't," Wendy told him. He really looked sick. "Look how fast they do it. It probably—won't even hurt." She was sweating but she spoke confidently.

The line inched down the aisle. Nelson had both hands in his mouth. Tears streamed down his cheeks.

"There's my sister," Wendy said, hoping to take his mind off fainting. "It's her turn." Denise winced as she received her shot. "Denise always makes faces. She's such a show-off."

Instead of following the students up the other aisle, Denise worked her way backward through the line to Wendy.

"It didn't hurt, did it?" Wendy asked her sister quickly, before Denise could say her arm killed her.

Denise noticed Nelson staring at her with enormous eyes. "Nah. I've had worse bee stings. In fact, it tickled. I'd have another one, but they won't let me."

Wendy giggled nervously.

"You can have mine," Nelson snuffled.

Denise patted his shoulder. "It'll be okay."

"Then it does hurt!" Nelson screamed. *"I knew you were lying!"*

"No, it doesn't," Denise said hastily. "Not really. I was just—I have to go back to class." She ran up the aisle.

"It's going to hurt!" Nelson wailed.

Mrs. Boggs left her place in the line. "What's going on here?" she asked Wendy. Nelson was crying too hard to answer.

"Nelson's scared," she answered for him. "He said he was going to faint. Does he have to have his shot today?"

Mrs. Boggs bit her lip. "I'm afraid he does. Nelson, honey," she said to him. "We all have to have this shot. You don't want to get polio, do you?"

"*Yes I do!*" he screeched. "I'd rather have polio than be stabbed with a needle! Please don't make me get a shot!"

By now everyone was looking at him, even the little kids.

"Listen to the sissypants," Wayne Supinger jeered.

"Wayne, be quiet," Mrs. Boggs ordered. Wayne shut up. "Nelson, come to the front with me. I'll stay right with you."

He didn't budge. When Mrs. Boggs took him by the wrist, he shrieked, "I want Wendy to come with me!"

"Of course Wendy can come with you." Their teacher led them both past the crying first and second graders to the front of the line. She said to the doctor, "This child cannot wait any longer. Let's get his vaccination over with before he makes himself sick."

Nelson dug in his heels and screamed even louder. *"No-no-no-no-no!"* His whole body was tense as he clung to the edge of the table. No one could move him.

Wendy was frightened, too. She'd much rather be way back in the line where she had been. But Nelson was truly scared. More scared than she was. Then Wendy had an idea. Maybe if Nelson saw it didn't hurt *her*, he wouldn't be so terrified.

"I'll go first," she spoke up.

"There's a brave girl," the nurse said. "Come right over, honey."

Wendy went over to the nurse, who rolled up her sleeve and dabbed a soaked cotton ball over a spot just below her shoulder. The cotton smelled of something that made her nose burn.

The doctor approached with his needle. Nelson peered around Mrs. Boggs, his eyes like dinner plates. Wendy put on a big grin. No matter what, she would keep grinning.

The needle hurt just like she knew it would and it hurt longer than a second. But she managed to grin through the whole thing. When the nurse pasted a Band-Aid on her arm, the grin became real. It was over! And she didn't even cry!

"Now it's your turn," Wendy coaxed Nelson.

Nelson was very pale, but at least he had stopped yelling. Mrs. Boggs and the nurse guided him over to the doctor. He moved stiffly, like a robot. Mrs. Boggs held his hand while the nurse rubbed his other arm with a cotton ball. The doctor talked softly as he jabbed the needle in Nelson's arm.

Nelson went limp.

The nurse caught him. Wendy ran forward, but the nurse commanded, "Stay back. Give him air."

Nelson opened his eyes, blinking. "Is it over?" he said feebly.

Mrs. Boggs smoothed his hair. "Yes, Nelson. It's all over." The doctor examined him and decided Nelson hadn't actually fainted. He could go lie down in the clinic for a while.

"I'm taking this child downstairs," Mrs. Boggs said firmly. "What he needs is a good cup of hot chocolate. Wendy, you come, too." She went over and asked Miss Kline, the other third grade teacher, to watch her class a few minutes.

With Nelson between them, Wendy and Mrs. Boggs left the auditorium. As they passed their class, everyone stared at them.

"Nelson fainted," Wendy heard Regina say importantly.

"He fainted?" Wayne repeated wonderingly. "Passed out cold? Boy, I never knew anybody to keel over in school before. What a great trick!"

Wendy could tell that Wayne was impressed. Maybe now Wayne would stop calling Nelson "sissypants."

Downstairs in the cafeteria, Wendy and Nelson sat at one of the big empty tables. Mrs. Boggs brought them steaming mugs of hot chocolate that she'd asked the cafeteria ladies to make just for them. She also brought them squares of gingerbread fresh from the oven. The gingerbread was today's dessert.

"I have to go back," Mrs. Boggs said. "Stay here as long as you need to."

"Thanks," Nelson said. To Wendy he added, "Thanks for coming with me. I would have fainted dead away without you."

119

"I didn't do anything," Wendy said. But she felt good. And she felt very grown-up, eating alone in the cafeteria.

She and Nelson ate their gingerbread. When they were finished, they peeled off one corner of their Band-Aids to look at their vaccinations. Wendy saw only the tiniest red mark, and that was fading quickly.

"Know what?" she said.

"What?" Nelson replied.

"We get to have our Halloween party early."

"Even better," Nelson said. "We're going to have two Halloween parties!"

It *had* been an exciting day, after all.

CHAPTER SEVEN

Sharing

The first week in November, there were only two air raid drills. Wendy was getting better at pretending to be a turtle. But she still hated the *whoop-whoop* of the siren.

On Thursday, the day of the second air raid drill, Wendy decided to talk to her father about it.

Mr. Fletcher was watching the evening

news. Denise was watching, too, for her current events class. She lay on her stomach in front of the TV, writing something now and then in her notebook.

Wendy sat beside her father on the sofa. She could hear her mother putting pans away in the kitchen. That was a nice, homey sound, not like the blare of sirens. "Daddy, do you have some earplugs I can have?"

"What do you want earplugs for?" her father wanted to know.

"So I won't have to listen to that awful siren."

Without turning around, Denise said, "She means the air raid siren. We had another drill today."

"It hurts my ears," Wendy said.

Her father put his arm around her. "I know it's loud, but you have to hear it. The siren is a warning of possible danger."

"Are we having a war?" Wendy asked.

"America and Russia don't get along," Mr. Fletcher explained. "The two countries don't talk to each other, but each side keeps building rockets with bombs on them. It's called a Cold War. No actual fighting . . . yet."

Wendy pictured soldiers flinging snowballs at each other. That's what a Cold War meant to her. It seemed silly, like a snowball fight.

"How come we don't get along with Russia?" she asked her sister. Wendy had no idea where Russia was. It must be across the ocean, like Germany.

"Because," Denise replied. "The Russians are different."

Was that any reason to have a war? Wendy wondered. She didn't know any Russians. In fact, she didn't know anybody who wasn't an American. She wondered what a Russian girl her age would look like. Would she have brown hair and bangs like Wendy? If she met a Russian girl, she hoped she would get along fine with her.

▪▪▪▪▪▪▪▪▪▪▪

The next afternoon, Mrs. Boggs handed out big sheets of drawing paper. "Art time," she said. "Draw a picture about fall or Thanksgiving or whatever you want. Be creative."

Wendy got out her crayons. She loved art time. It was her favorite subject. She knew exactly what she'd draw.

Because the teacher gave them almost an hour, Wendy drew the biggest, fanciest Birdland ever. The tree sprouted thirteen main branches and lots of little branches, each lined with birdhouse buildings. She used every crayon in her box. There were orange birds, yellow birds, blue-green birds, spotted birds, and striped birds. All the birds were gloriously different.

She was working so hard that she didn't see her teacher pause by her desk.

"Why, Wendy," Mrs. Boggs exclaimed. "What a wonderful picture! It's like the one on your Best Work folder, only bigger. You must share it with the class. Right now!"

Wendy's heart stalled. Get up in front of the class and show her drawing. It wasn't the same as the things the other kids had shared: a rock collection, chopsticks from the Far East, a live chinchilla. Her drawing wasn't even as nice as the blue jay feather she had found and threw away that time. Who cared about a picture?

"It's a neat drawing," Kristy said.

Regina turned around in her seat. "Yeah, we want to see it."

"Show everybody how good you can draw," Nelson urged.

Some friends they were! Wendy thought. They wanted her to be laughed at!

Reluctantly she went to the front of the room. She stood nervously by Mrs. Boggs's desk, holding her drawing in front of her like a shield. Her mouth felt like cotton.

"Say something," Wayne called. He looked so safe, sitting at his own desk.

"Wayne," Mrs. Boggs warned. "I will not tolerate rudeness. Let's give Wendy our undivided attention."

Everyone sat quietly in their chairs. All eyes were on Wendy. She gulped. Kristy and Regina smiled encouragingly. Nelson gave her the thumbs-up sign. Wendy felt a little better.

"This is Birdland," she whispered.

"Can't hear you!" Wayne said.

"Wayne, one more word out of you and you'll write sentences," Mrs. Boggs said. To Wendy, she added, "Wendy, speak up so everyone can hear you."

"This is Birdland," Wendy began again. "It's—it's a place I made up. The birdhouses are schools and churches and stores. And houses, too. It's like a city for birds."

She glanced hopefully at her teacher. Was that enough? Could she sit down now?

"A whole world for birds," Mrs. Boggs commented. "Notice that Wendy's birds are all different. And they seem happy living together. Did you do that on purpose? Make the birds in your town different?" she asked Wendy.

Wendy wasn't sure how to answer that. Then she remembered what her father said. " 'If everybody was the same, what a dull place the world would be,' " she quoted.

"Very good! I wish a couple of world leaders could hear you. I'm very proud of you, Wendy. Thank you for sharing your picture with us." Mrs. Boggs clapped.

Soon the whole class was applauding, her friends—her three real friends—clapping louder than anybody. Wayne gave a two-finger whistle.

Wendy sat down, her cheeks flushed with pride. She'd done it! She stood up in front of the entire class and nobody laughed. She might even do it again sometime.

■■■■■■■■■■■

When Wendy and Denise got home, their mother met them at the door.

"Guess what?" she greeted. "I got a job! In your school cafeteria. I start Monday."

"You got a job in our school?" Denise repeated.

"Yes." Mrs. Fletcher beamed. "Isn't it

great? Now we won't have to pinch pennies."

Wendy had almost forgotten about the tight year. In fact, she had forgotten most of her old worries. She had been busy helping her friends, being a real friend herself.

"Does this mean we won't have a tight year anymore?" she asked.

Her mother rumpled her hair. "Wendy the worrywart! We won't be rich, but things won't be so tight."

"Then I can go on the trip to Richmond?" Denise said.

"And can I get new shoes?" Wendy asked. "I don't think my shoes are going to make it to Christmas."

"With my first paycheck," Mrs. Fletcher promised. "Didn't I tell you girls not to worry? Everything will be okay."

Wendy went outside with her sister.

Denise fetched the newspaper from the box. Wendy read the word RUSSIA in the headline.

"Are the Russians still mad at us?" she asked Denise. She was tired of pretending to be a turtle.

"I don't think we're friends with Russia yet," Denise said, crawling under the porch to get her ball.

"Will we ever be friends?" Wendy wondered. "I don't mind if they're different from us." She imagined everyone living together in a world like Birdland. Maybe someday.

Denise tossed her ball up on the roof over the porch. The ball hit the gutter, then bounced out. Denise caught it neatly.

Wendy wandered over to the grape arbor. The thick, gnarled vines were leafless. It would soon be winter. That meant snow! And snowball fights with her friends. Only, after their Cold War, they would still be friends.

Something bonked Wendy on the head, then bounced into the grape arbor.

Denise ran after her ball. "Sorry!" she said.

The ball had knocked some vines loose. Wendy saw something, a secret the vines had been hiding. A bird's nest rested snugly between the arbor post and the twisted vines. Wendy stood on tiptoe to peek inside.

The nest was perfectly round, a deep cup woven of straw, grass, and bits of string. The bottom was lined with soft gray feathers. How safe the baby birds must have felt in their snug little home!

Wendy was glad the birds were gone. It would have been awful if Denise's ball had landed on their house while they were still in it.

She looked back at her own house. It was made of bricks and shingles and wood. Her mother had painted the porch red to match the bricks and there were green chairs by the railing. Wendy often sat outside with her father to watch evening swallows. The gutter was bent from Denise's ball.

Her house was safe and snug, too. A good place to grow up, like the bird's nest. And yet . . . Wendy thought about the air raid drills. All of her worries weren't gone.

Denise chanted, "Ladies and jellybeans! I come before you to stand behind you to tell you something I know nothing about!"

Denise didn't sound worried, but Wendy knew the air raid drills scared her, too. Yet Denise went on, laughing, singing, playing ball.

Stretching, Wendy reached between the vines and gently worked the nest free. Holding the nest carefully, she headed across the yard. It wouldn't be as hard getting up in front of the class a second time, she decided. Especially since she had this great thing to share.

"Tickets are free, pay at the door," Wendy cried, taking up the speech where Denise left off. "Pull up a chair and sit on the floor." She finally got the words right!

She set the nest on the porch, then picked up a stick. Spinning in her sudden happiness, she wrote "Wendy F." in the air.

In cursive!

ABOUT THE AUTHOR

Candice F. Ransom is the author of more than two dozen contemporary novels for older readers. About *Ladies and Jellybeans*, her first novel published by Bradbury, she writes, "In books, the eight-year-old seems to be the forgotten child. I wanted to write a book for this age child, who is at a transitional time—no longer a baby but not yet an older kid. I chose to set my book in the late fifties because I believe the Cold War is worth knowing about, even though it is over. My own third-grade year—upon which this book is based—was fraught with worries, the little embarrassing things (not being able to tie my shoes or ride a bike), plus bigger worries. The Cuban missile crisis occurred around this time, and I sensed that the adults around me were afraid. So was I. Today, children still worry about little things, like learning to write cursive, and big things, like war. It's important for all generations to understand that these worries are ongoing third-grade concerns that are, unfortunately, unlikely to ever go away."